Rachel Isadora
I TOUCH

Greenwillow Books, New York

Library of Congress Cataloging in Publication Data

Isadora, Rachel.
I touch.
Summary: A very young child names
the things she touches.
1. Children's stories, American.
[1. Touch—Fiction.
2. Senses and sensation—Fiction]
I. Title.
PZ7.I763Iau 1985   [E]   84-13673
ISBN 0-688-04255-4
ISBN 0-688-04256-2 (lib. bdg.)

For Gillian Heather

I touch
my bear.
He's soft.

I touch Mommy.
She laughs.

I do
not
touch
the
cup.
It's hot.

I touch
my cereal.
It's gooey.

I touch
my cat.
She purrs.

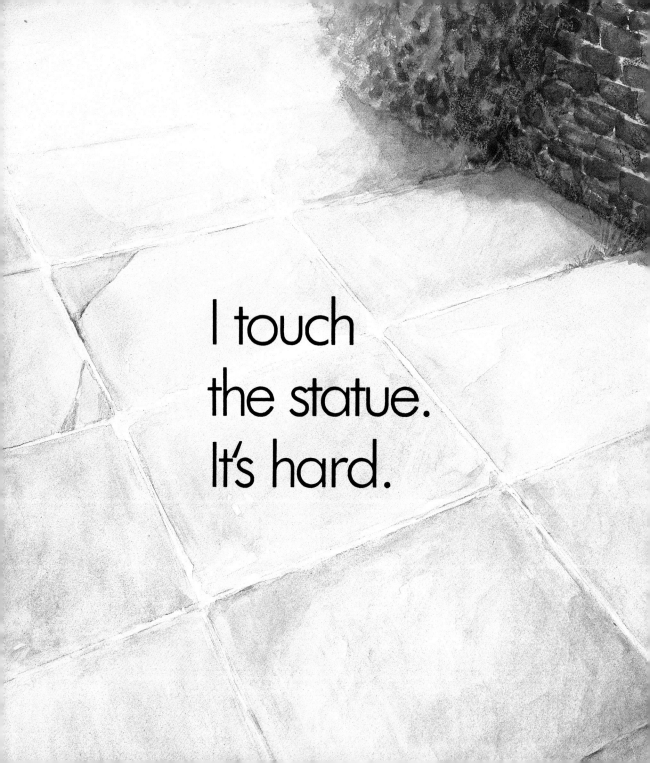

I touch
the statue.
It's hard.

I touch
the leaves.
Crunch, crunch.

I touch the
butterfly.
It flies away.

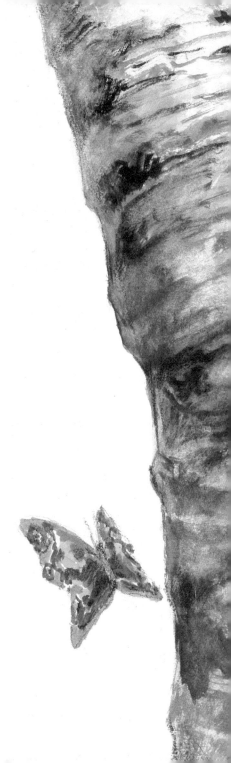

I touch
my lollipop.
It's sticky.

I touch
the sand.
It's rough.

I touch
the bubble.
It pops.

I touch
the newspaper.
It crinkles.

I touch
Daddy's beard.
It's scratchy.

I touch
my blanket.

Good night.